This Rio Chico book belongs to:

_____

# THE SUNhat

by Jennifer Ward

illustrated by Stephanie Roth Sisson

Rio CHiCo

Books for Children

Rio Chico, an imprint of Rio Nuevo Publishers®
P. O. Box 5250
Tucson, AZ 85703-0250
(520) 623-9558, www.rionuevo.com

Production Date: June, 2013
Printed by Guangzhou Yicai Printing Co., Ltd., Guangzhou, China
Job # J130531FC02

10  9  8  7  6  5  4  3  2  1      13  14  15  16  17  18  19  20

Library of Congress Cataloging-in-Publication Data

Ward, Jennifer, 1963-
  The sunhat / by Jennifer Ward ; Illustrated by Stephanie Roth Sisson.
      pages cm
  Summary: Rosa has a wonderful hat that fits her just right, but when the wind blows it away the
hat shelters a wide variety of desert creatures from a storm.
  ISBN 978-1-933855-78-3 (hardcover : alk. paper)
  [1. Hats—Fiction. 2. Desert animals—Fiction. 3. Storms—Fiction. 4. Deserts—Fiction.]
  I. Sisson, Stephanie Roth, illustrator. II. Title.
  PZ7.W21322Sun 2013
  [E]—dc23
                                    2013002030

To Suzi
      — J.W.

To Tom and Kristine Hare.
I'm lucky to have you. Much love,
      — S.R.S.

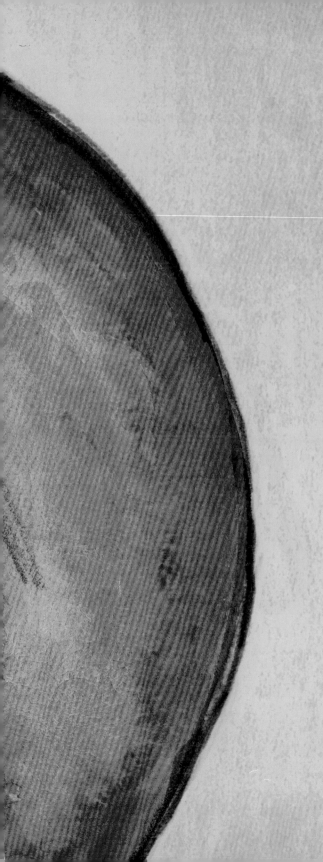

Rosa wore a sunhat
red as rubies, soft as sand.
It fit snug upon her head and
shaded her freckles from the sun.

Sometimes a hat fits just like that.

One morning, a wind blew
across the hot, dry desert.
It swirled from one place
and twirled toward another.
It passed by Rosa, and

# WHOOSH!

Just like that, away flew her hat.

"Oh no!" cried Rosa.
But away it blew, and Rosa
had to hurry to school.

Way out in the desert, exactly where the wind
decided to drop it, a mouse found the sunhat.

The sun above sizzled. The ground below baked.
Mouse squeaked under for a nice, cool break.

Jackrabbit hopped by, stopping to nibble at a prickly pear patch.

The heat rose.
Dark clouds began to form.
Must find shelter...
**Monsoon Storm!**

Move over, mouse.

Share with hare!

On his way from here to there, roadrunner raced by.

Skies flashed. Loud crash. Lightning, thunder!

Hurry under!

Move over, mouse.

Share, hare.

Make room for roadrunner!

Along trudged tortoise.
Pitter-patter!
Raindrops splatter.

Move over, mouse.

Share, hare.

Make room, roadrunner!

Amble under, tortoise!

Mama, Papa, and baby quail quit their search
for seeds as the tumbleweeds tumbled
and the skies above rumbled.

Move over, mouse.

Share, hare.

Make room, roadrunner!

Amble aside, tortoise.

Take cover quick, quail!

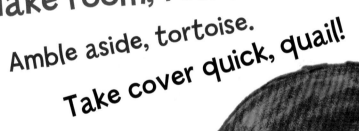

Rain was whipping.
Fox was dripping.

Move over, mouse.
Share, hare.
Make room, roadrunner.
Amble aside, tortoise.
Be quick, quail.
Find a spot, fox!

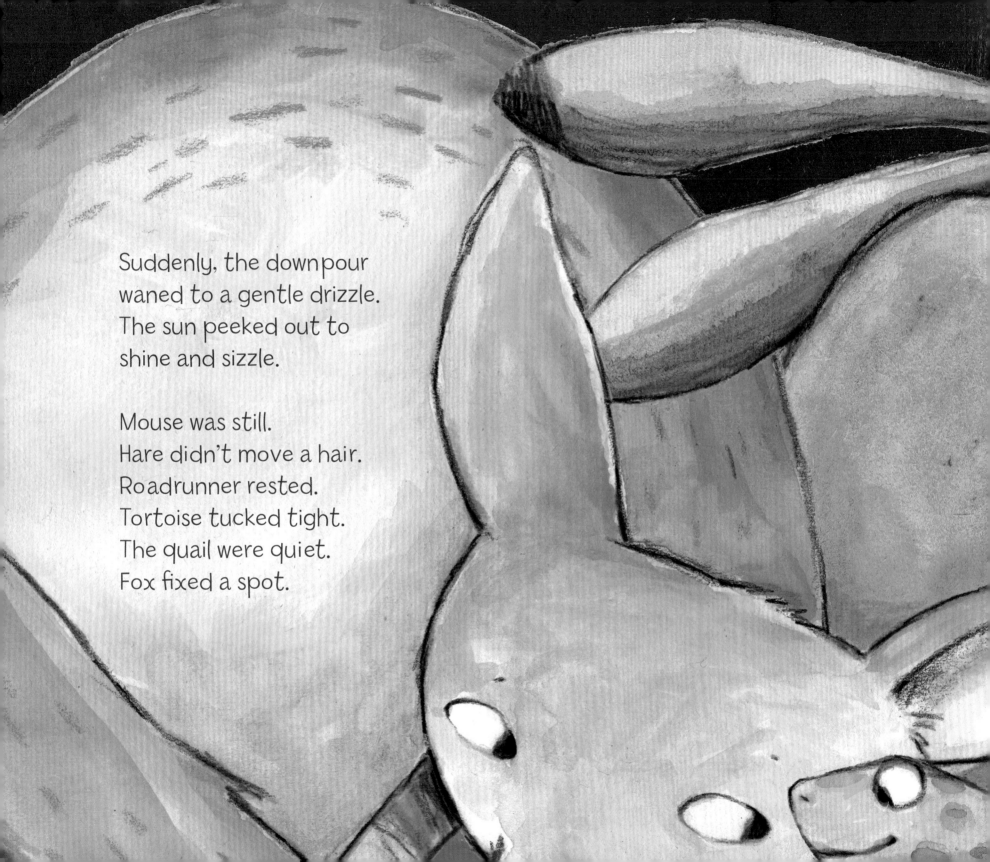

Suddenly, the downpour
waned to a gentle drizzle.
The sun peeked out to
shine and sizzle.

Mouse was still.
Hare didn't move a hair.
Roadrunner rested.
Tortoise tucked tight.
The quail were quiet.
Fox fixed a spot.

All was snug beneath the sunhat.

At that very moment,
a wind blew across the desert.
It swirled from one place and
twirled toward another, and

WHOOSH!

just like that,
away flew that hat.

Grumble. Stumble.
Animals tumble!
See them scatter
from the sunhat stretched fatter!

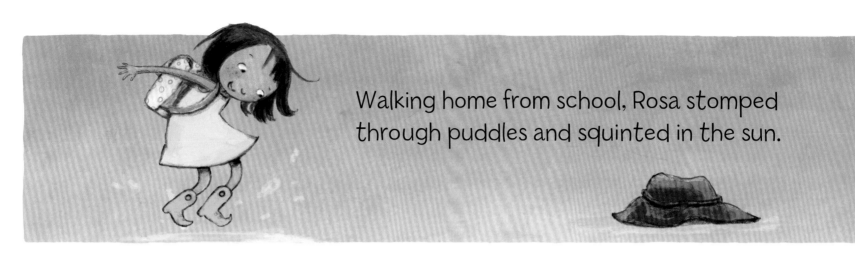

Walking home from school, Rosa stomped through puddles and squinted in the sun.

On her path,
exactly where the wind
decided to drop it,
lay her sunhat.

"Could it be?"
she wondered.

Rosa picked it up and gave it a few good shakes.
It was still red as rubies, soft as sand.

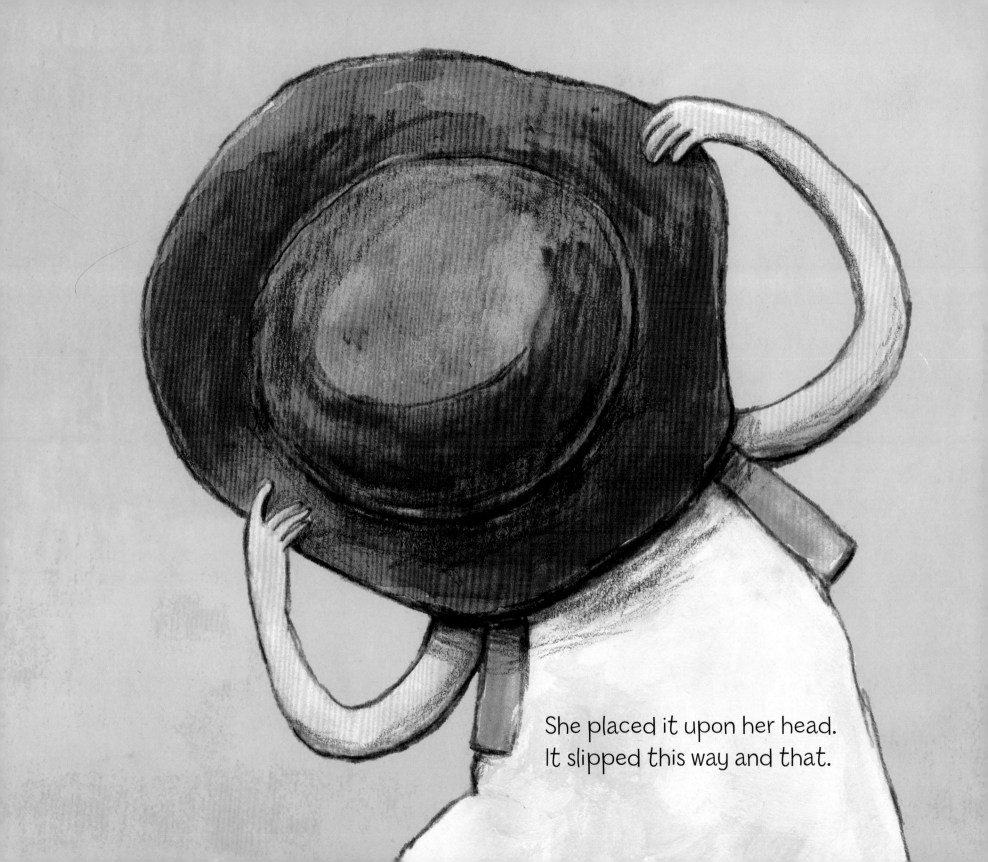

She placed it upon her head.
It slipped this way and that.

Because sometimes
a hat fits just
       like
     that.